PIES

Wilma Riley · Sheldon Cohen

Coteau Books 1991

Book design by Shelley Sopher, Coteau Books.

Typeset by Lines and Letters.

Printed and bound in Hong Kong.

The publisher gratefully acknowledges the
financial assistance of the Saskatchewan Arts Board
and the Canada Council.

Canadian Cataloguing in Publication Data

Riley, Wilma
Pies

ISBN 1-55050-021-X

I. Cohen, Sheldon, 1949-. II. Title.

PS8585.I549P5 1991   jC813/.54   C91-097148-X
PZ7.R554Pi 1991

C O T E A U   B O O K S
401–2206 Dewdney Avenue
Regina, Saskatchewan
S4R 1H3

Wilma dedicates her story to neighbours, cows and the fields we have to cross.

Sheldon dedicates his illustrations to all the neighbours he has argued with.

Two women lived across the road from one another. They might as well have lived on separate planets, they were so different. Mary grew a large garden and kept a cow in a field near the two houses. She loved fresh milk and cream and fresh vegetables from her garden. Maybe she would have liked to live on a farm.

Her neighbour, Elena, liked to have a very clean house and yard. She liked to dress up and go shopping. Baking and cooking were things she did well. She could crochet beautifully, and she filled her house with pretty things she had made. Maybe she would have liked to live in a city.

No matter where each would have liked to live, they both lived in a little village just outside a city. In spite of being neighbours, they did not know each other very well. As far as Elena was concerned, she wished her neighbour and, even more, her neighbour's cow were on the moon.

One day they had a terrible fight.

It started after Elena had taken a short-cut across the field and got her shoes dirty.

"The dirty cow, the dirty cow!" Elena looked out at her neighbour, Mary, as she was leading the cow home.

"Oh I hate to see that cow! It's cow here, cow there. Everywhere, cow!"

"What are you talking about, Mamma?" asked Peter, Elena's husband. "The cow is always in the field."

"But there shouldn't be a cow at all! This is not a farm. This village is almost a city. She has no right to keep a cow!"

"The cow does no harm and Mary brings you butter and cream, sometimes."

"I don't want the butter and cream!" Elena shouted. "I want a nice, clean house, a nice clean sidewalk and no smell of cows! Look!" She pointed at Peter's shoes. "Those shoes should be outside. You know none of us may wear shoes in the house!"

"Yes, yes, Mamma. Be calm now. I'm taking them off."

"Oh I am fed up! I'm going to tell her what I think of that cow!" Elena marched out in spite of Peter's protests. She went over to Mary's house.

Mary was talking to Bossie, her cow. Mary was going to milk the cow.

"Mary!" Elena waved her hands. "Yoo hoo! I want to talk about the cow!"

"Oh hello, Elena." Mary turned with a smile. "How are you?"

"I can't stand this cow any longer!" Elena said loudly. "It's not a farm here. Look what a mess she has made in this field. Look!" Elena pointed at the cow manure. "Cow dung here! Cow dung there! I can't walk to the store without getting my shoes dirty. Today the cow chased me!"

"No! The cow is always good. Why don't you walk on the sidewalk?" Mary felt angry that Elena would say bad things about the cow. Mary remembered that Elena didn't mind the gifts of cream and butter. Elena worried too much about her house. "You shouldn't be so fussy about your house!"

"*You* should be fussy! It's dirty to keep a cow in this field. You're dirty too!"

"I am dirty? Me?" Mary was angry now. She had a clean house. Just because she kept a cow, Elena was calling her dirty. "I'll show you who is dirty! You big-shot city lady!" She gave Elena a push.

Elena slipped and fell into the cow manure.

"Aihh!" Elena shrieked with horror and picked up some manure and threw it at Mary. "You pig! You pig!" She shouted.

"Pig? Me? I'll show you who is a pig!" Mary picked up some manure and threw it at Elena. Elena ducked but some of it landed in her hair and that was too much. She ran back home. Mary shook her fist at her.

"Bring me some soap and water!" Elena shouted to Peter and her two daughters who were watching out the window with shocked faces.

Poor Elena! She hated mud. But cow manure! She cleaned everything. She had a hot bath. That night she dreamed of cows and cow manure and angry neighbours and neighbours who laughed at her and called her "big-shot city lady."

Elena could not forget the fight. She watched out the window. Mary continued to lead her cow to the field. She talked to the beast. She petted the cow. Elena thought she looked at her house and was giving her dirty looks.

Mary and Elena had come to Canada from different countries. A few years before, their old countries had been at war with each other. Now this was all mixed up in Elena's mind with the fight about the cow and Elena went around muttering awful things about Mary and Mary's old country, too.

Day after day, Elena thought about the fight. She neglected her cleaning. She neglected herself. Peter was sorry for her, but what could he do?

Her daughters giggled and whispered. They thought it was funny. "Cow pies! Cow pies!" Elena heard them whispering.

Then one day Elena got a nasty idea.

She would get revenge on Mary and she would seem to be perfectly sweet about it. Then maybe she could forget the whole thing.

"Tell Mary's husband that I'm sorry about the fight and tell him I want Mary to come for coffee day after tomorrow," she said to Peter one day.

Peter did as Elena asked. The next day he said, "Mary said she would come tomorrow. I'm so happy, Mamma, that you are over your anger. Mary is happy too."

Elena wasn't over her anger and furthermore she didn't believe Mary was either.

That night Elena got out her recipe book. "Butter Tarts . . . no," she muttered. "Chocolate Cake . . . no . . . Mincemeat Pie . . . ah that's it. Nice and spicy."

When everyone was asleep Elena crept out of the house and brought some fresh cow manure home in a little pail.

The next morning she made the pie and put some of the cow manure in it. You couldn't taste it because of the sugar and spice and raisins and other good things in the recipe. When it was cooked all the germs were killed too. Elena didn't want to make Mary sick. She wanted the satisfaction of seeing Mary eat the cow dung. After, perhaps she would tell her. It would be good, Elena thought, to see that look of surprise and alarm on her neighbour's face. Let her see what it meant to have a cow! Yes, perhaps, she would tell her . . . after.

"Ah, it smells delicious," Elena said when it was cooked.

When Mary arrived at Elena's door she took her shoes off before she entered.

She handed Elena a bowl covered with a snowy white cloth. "Here, I brought you some fresh butter. I hope you are well? Thank you for asking me to come over."

"Oh yes, very . . . very well. You shouldn't have . . . you know . . . brought the butter." Elena was a little embarrassed. Mary looked so clean. She was smiling and so polite. It was probably a trick, Elena decided. "Come in. We'll have coffee. It is cool for this time of year," she said and led Mary to the living room.

"Oh yes. All July has been rainy and cold. Not like before."

They sat down at the lovely tea-table Elena had set. Mary admired Elena's crocheting. "The doilies are so pretty and I can't do that work. My eyes are not so good."

Elena was concentrating on making her voice sound natural. "Would you like some pie?"

"Yes, please, it smells wonderful."

Elena cut a generous slice for Mary. "I ate almost a whole pie already, so I'll only have a cookie. This is my favourite pie."

"What is it called?"

"Mincemeat but there's no meat in it."

Mary took a bite of it. Her eyes lit up. "It's very good. How do you make it?"

"With apples and raisins, spices and sugar."

Mary continued to eat the pie. Elena thought she would get satisfaction to see Mary eating the cow-dung pie, but somehow she didn't feel happy at all. Mary was a hard-working woman. She trusted Elena just as a child is trusting. Elena had a very unpleasant feeling somewhere in her throat as she watched Mary eat the pie, forkful by forkful.

"I'm sorry I said those things to you," Mary said between mouthfuls of pie, "and getting angry and throwing . . . I'll bring you cream and butter. The cow can't help making manure."

"I shouldn't have acted like that either," Elena said. Mary was finished her pie. She looked hungrily toward the pie dish. "Would you like some cookies?" Elena said and pushed the plate of cookies towards her.

"No thanks." Mary's eyes were on the pie. Elena knew that it was her duty as a hostess to offer Mary more pie.

"Will you have some more pie, then?" Elena said in a high, strained voice. Now she was feeling awful. She didn't want Mary to eat more pie but she couldn't tell her why. As long as Mary never knew what was in it there could be no harm in it for her.

"Oh yes, please. It's so sweet and spicy."

Elena put another piece of pie on Mary's plate.

"Have you seen the new statue of Holy Mother in our church?" Mary asked. Elena hadn't because she was too ashamed to go to church after the fight, afraid of the laughter of her neighbours. "I always pray to Holy Mother," Mary said. "I think she is a bit like me. She's poor. She works hard. And she knows what it is like to have worries about her child."

Elena looked at Mary. Mary was smiling. Could Mary have troubles with her daughter? Did she know how Elena's daughters were laughing and saying, "Cow pies?" But no, Mary was just joking.

"Aha, it's true." Elena suddenly laughed so much she had to catch her breath. "Everybody worries about their children."

Elena now felt very ashamed. Mary had the same troubles as she. How could she think Mary was trying to be mean about the cow? Elena knew what she must do to make it up to her.

"I think I'll have a piece of pie, too," she said to Mary and she dished out a generous slice for herself as well.

"I can't let my neighbour eat alone."

Silently, Elena prayed over her pie. "Holy Mother, forgive me that I hated my poor neighbour and help me swallow this pie."

Suddenly she felt light and wonderful and filled with a strange happiness. She got gooseflesh just as she did sometimes when the priest spoke about miracles. She ate her pie. It tasted like mincemeat pie, nothing else.

"It's a wonderful pie," Mary said. "I think we'll be friends now. Can you give me the recipe? But I'll never make it as good as you."

"Maybe better," Elena said. "We all have our own ways to cook, our own secrets."